Carlos & Carmen

The Perfect Piñatas

by Kirsten McDonald
illustrated by Erika Meza

Calico Kid

An Imprint of Magic Wagon
abdopublishing.com

For Erika so that she can have lots of fun creating the perfect piñatas —KKM

For the whole team in ABDO (Candice, Tina, Heidi, Meg!!), who became dear friends and helped create this wonderful family. —EM

abdopublishing.com

Published by Magic Wagon, a division of ABDO, PO Box 398166, Minneapolis, Minnesota 55439. Copyright © 2017 by Abdo Consulting Group, Inc. International copyrights reserved in all countries. No part of this book may be reproduced in any form without written permission from the publisher. Calico Kid™ is a trademark and logo of Magic Wagon.

Printed in the United States of America, North Mankato, Minnesota.
102016
012017

Written by Kirsten McDonald
Illustrated by Erika Meza
Edited by Heidi M.D. Elston
Design Contributors: Christina Doffing & Candice Keimig

Publisher's Cataloging in Publication Data

Names: McDonald, Kirsten, author. I Meza, Erika, illustrator.
Title: The perfect piñatas / by Kirsten McDonald ; illustrated by Erika Meza.
Description: Minneapolis, MN : Magic Wagon, 2017. I Series: Carlos & Carmen
Summary: Carlos and Carmen's Abuelita has come to visit. She joins the twins, Mamá, and
   Papá as they go from store to store, searching for the perfect piñatas. When they finally find
   them, the twins fall in love with their new piñata pets. They don't want to smash them!
   Luckily, Abuelita knows just what to do.
Identifiers: LCCN 2016947654 I ISBN 9781624021831 (lib. bdg.) I ISBN 9781624022432
   (ebook) I ISBN 9781624022739 (Read-to-me ebook)
Subjects: LCSH: Hispanic American families--Juvenile fiction. I Twins--Juvenile fiction. I Brothers
   and sisters--Juvenile fiction. I Grandmothers--Juvenile fiction. I Piñatas--Juvenile fiction.
Classification: DDC [E]--dc23
LC record available at http://lccn.loc.gov/2016947654

Table of Contents

Chapter 1
Shopping

Carlos and Carmen held their grandmother's hands. They were shopping for the perfect piñatas.

EXIT

5

In the first store, they saw turtle piñatas and train piñatas. They saw princess piñatas and pony piñatas. They even saw piñatas shaped like pineapples.

"Look at these wonderful piñatas, mis nietos," said Abuelita.

Carlos and Carmen fluffed the ruffly paper on the piñatas. They turned each piñata this way and that. But they could not find the perfect piñatas.

In the second store, they saw rocket piñatas and rainbow piñatas. They saw pig piñatas and parrot piñatas. They even saw piñatas shaped like tacos.

"I think this is the perfect piñata," said Papá, holding up a star piñata.

Carlos and Carmen looked at the star piñata.

"It is big and shiny," said Carmen. "But I'm not sure it's perfect."

"Yo tampoco," agreed Carlos.

"How about this one?" asked Mamá, holding up a seahorse piñata.

"It is big and happy," said Carlos. "But I'm not sure it's perfect, either."

At the third store, there were piñatas on the ceiling. There were piñatas on the floor. There were piñatas on the shelves and piñatas in the bins.

And in the corner, the twins found just what they were looking for.

"¡Mira!" shouted Carlos. "A green dinosaurio like the one on the poster in my room!"

"¡Mira!" shouted Carmen. "A cute elephant like the one on the poster in my room!"

Carlos looked at Carmen. Carmen looked at Carlos. "Are you thinking what I'm thinking?" they said. And because they were twins, they were.

Chapter 2
A Piñata Problem

At home, the twins and the perfect piñatas did everything together. They played hide-and-seek and soccer. And, they all took turns on the tire swing.

At supper, Carmen shared her chair with her elephant piñata. Carlos shared his chair with his dinosaur piñata.

And at bedtime, Carmen tucked her piñata into her sleeping bag.

"Good night, Ellie," she said.

Carlos tucked his piñata into his sleeping bag.

"Good night, Dino," he said.

Murr-ahh, said Spooky. She thought the piñatas were pretty perfect too.

"I'm glad we found the perfect piñatas," said Carmen.

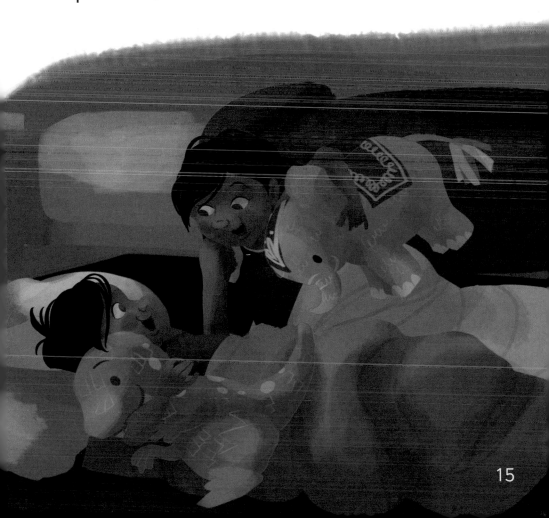

"Yo también," said Carlos. "Except I don't want to smash them."

"Yo tampoco," said Carmen. "But I do want candy and toys falling from the sky for our cumpleaños."

"Yo también," agreed Carlos.

The twins thought about their piñata problem.

"Maybe we could shake the candy and toys out," said Carlos.

"That would not be exciting," said Carmen as she yawned.

"And it would not be surprising," said Carlos with a yawn.

The twins thought some more. They yawned some more. Then they both fell asleep dreaming about birthdays.

Chapter 3
Little Doors

Carlos and Carmen poked at their pancakes. Spooky poked at one of Ellie's long, paper tassels.

19

"Mis hijos," said Papá, "why are you so sad?"

Carlos said, "We found the perfect piñatas for our cumpleaños."

Carmen said, "And we want candy and toys falling from the sky."

"But we don't want Dino to get smashed," said Carlos.

"And we don't want Ellie to get smashed," said Carmen.

"What you need is a bunch of cintas," said Abuelita.

"How can a bunch of ribbons help us?" Carmen asked.

"Just get me a roll of cinta, some scissors, and some tape," said Abuelita. "I know just how to fix this problem."

In no time at all, the twins found ribbon, scissors, and tape.

The twins watched Abuelita cut doors in the bottoms of both piñatas. They watched her tape ribbons to the inside of each piñata's door.

Nine ribbons had tiny pieces of tape. One ribbon got lots and lots of tape.

"¡Mira!" said Abuelita. "These nine cintas will come loose when they are pulled. But the one with lots of tape will open the piñata's door."

"And candy can fall from the sky," said Carmen.

"And nobody will smash our perfect piñatas," added Carlos.

"Let's try it!" the twins said.

Chapter 4
Perfect Piñatas

Abeulita held Ellie upside down.
Carlos dropped bouncy balls inside
the little door. Carmen dropped in
handfuls of peanuts still in their shells.

Papa stood on the stairs and held Ellie up high.

"Both of you close your eyes," Abuelita said to the twins. "Turn around five times. No peeking, mis nietos."

Carlos and Carmen closed their eyes. They turned around and around.

"I'm dizzy," said Carlos.

"Yo también," said Carmen, holding out her arms for balance.

"Keep your eyes closed and choose a cinta," said Abuelita.

Carlos and Carmen swept their arms through the air.

"I found one," said Carmen, and she yanked the ribbon. Nothing happened.

"My turn," said Carlos, and he yanked a ribbon. Nothing happened.

"Grab another cinta," said Mamá. "And no peeking, mis hijos."

Carlos grabbed another ribbon and pulled. This time, the ribbon opened the little door in the piñata. Peanuts and bouncy balls poured out.

"Hooray!" shouted Carlos, scooping up peanuts.

"Double hooray!" shouted Carmen as she chased a bouncy ball.

Murr-uhhh, added Spooky as she batted balls and pounced on peanuts.

"Thank you, Abuelita!" the twins shouted.

"You solved our piñata problem," said Carmen.

"Now our piñatas are perfect," said Carlos.

The twins and the perfect piñatas gave Abuelita big, squeezy hugs. Then everybody got busy planning the best birthdays ever.

Spanish to English

Abuelita – Grandma

cintas – ribbons

cumpleaños – birthday

dinosaurio – dinosaur

Mamá – Mommy

¡Mira! – Look!

mis hijos – my children

mis nietos – my grandchildren

Papá – Daddy

yo también – me too

yo tampoco – me neither